Modern Panchatantra

Stories to Read, Imagine and Colour

Chirag Arora

For the deep love
that stories bring to our lives.

As you turn the pages and color the scenes, may you
experience the joy and excitement that only a great
story can offer.

Contents

Introduction

Welcome to the Magical World of Modern Panchatantra!

Are you ready for a fun adventure? In this special coloring book, we'll meet the wise animal characters from the classic Panchatantra stories, but this time, they're exploring the cool world of technology!

When I was a kid, I loved reading the thrilling tales of Panchatantra. They taught me how to make smart choices and be a good friend. Now, I want to share these stories with you, but with a twist! In this book, we'll see how our favorite animal friends handle gadgets, computers, and all the digital stuff we use today.

You'll find some old stories that might remind you of the ones your parents read, plus brand-new adventures made just for our world. And guess what? You can color in all the pictures as you go!

So, grab your crayons and join me on this exciting journey. Let's dive into these tales and learn how to be wise and kind, just like the characters in the stories.

I hope you'll love reading and coloring these stories as much as I loved creating them. Let's head to Aranya Van and enjoy the adventure!

Chirag Arora

Chapter 1

The WhatsApp Crow and the Mischievous Monkey

Once upon a time, in the bustling forest of Aranya Van, there lived a clever crow named Chitvan and a mischievous monkey named Manu. Chitvan was known far and wide for his wisdom, while Manu was infamous for his pranks and tricks.

Chitvan belonged to a WhatsApp group of forest animals managed by Manu. As he read the chat, Chitvan discovered that Manu was behind all the chaos. Manu's messages contained fake news and tricks, such as spreading false rumors like "The river's poisoned! Don't

WhatsApp
is like a secret clubhouse
where you can chat, play, and
share stories with your best
pals, no matter how far away
they are!

drink!" This caused animals to avoid the river, leading to dehydration and illness.

One day, Manu started telling everyone in the forest about magical fruits that grew in the forest. These fruits were said to be the most delicious and special treats ever. The animals got very excited and began searching everywhere for these magical fruits. They forgot about their regular food and started causing a lot of confusion in the forest.

Seeing the chaos unfold, Chitvan decided to take action. He created a new WhatsApp account and pretended to be an innocent animal who had found the magical fruits. He thanked Manu for revealing the secret and even gave him directions to where the fruits were supposed to be.

Excited by the possibility of his prank coming true, Manu eagerly followed

Oh no!
That's so many bees! How did
Manu get into such a sticky
situation?

the directions. But instead of finding delicious fruits, he stumbled upon a swarm of angry bees! The bees, furious at Manu's intrusion, attacked him with painful stings. Manu tried to escape, but the bees left him in a sorry state with painful bites.

Manu realized his mistake and felt remorse for causing trouble in the forest. He apologized to the other animals and promised to bring joy without harm. From then on, Manu learned the importance of kindness and thinking before playing pranks on others. And with Chitvan's wisdom guiding him, Manu became a better and more considerate member of the forest community.

The story of Manu
teaches us to be kind and
think about others' feelings
before playing pranks!

Chapter 2

The Zoom Owl
and the
Carefree Bear

In the heart of the dense jungle of Aranya Van, there lived a wise owl named Guruji. He wanted to share his knowledge with all the animals, so he organized a special online course called "Jungle Survival Skills" on Zoom. The course was conducted online, allowing animals from distant parts of the jungle to participate without the need for physical travel.

Among the eager participants was a carefree bear named Bholu. He never bothered to turn on his video during class and often got distracted by other

Zoom
is like a special window
where friends gather to see
each other and play together,
even when they're
far away!

things, like munching on honey instead of paying attention. Bholu thought he could get away with it because the exams were virtual and nobody would catch him cheating.

During one of the virtual classes, Guruji confronted him about his lack of engagement, "Bholu, it seems you're not fully focused during the classes. Is there something on your mind?" Guruji asked. Bholu sheepishly replied, "Well, Guruji, I find the classes a bit boring". Guruji tried to emphasise the importance of learning but Bholu was not ready to listen. Bholu continued to disengage and even started preparing for cheating by watching Youtube videos on "How to cheat during virtual exams"

But when exam time came, Guruji surprised everyone by announcing that there would be no virtual exam. Instead, they had to demonstrate their survival skills in real life scenarios.

It seems like Guruji has a plan, but will he allow Bholu to cheat during tests?

Bholu's confidence crumbled because he couldn't cheat like he planned. During the test, all the animals showed what they had learned, but Bholu struggled and failed.

Realizing his mistake, Bholu had to retake the course and the exams. He learned the hard way that cheating doesn't pay off. From then on, he participated actively in his classes and never tried to cheat again. It was a tough lesson, but Bholu emerged wiser and more honest than before.

The story of Bholu teaches us to be honest, work hard, and learn with integrity, both in person and online!

Chapter 3

The Amazon Deer and the Shopaholic Zebra

In the lush jungle of Aranya Van, there lived a striped zebra named Zaheer and a wise deer named Daya. They were the best of friends and went on many adventures together.

One day, Zaheer discovered the Amazon app and fell in love with the idea of online shopping. He couldn't resist the excitement of ordering all sorts of things, big and small, essential and not-so-essential. Every delivery brought him joy as he eagerly opened his packages.

But as time passed, Zaheer's shopping

The Amazon
is like a treasure chest
where you can find anything
you want to buy, right at your
fingertips!

habit started to get out of hand. His home became cluttered with things he didn't really need.

Daya, noticing this, gently voiced her concerns. She believed in owning only what was truly necessary and valued experiences over material possessions. Zaheer laughed off Daya's worries, insisting that his purchases made him happy. However, Daya remained worried.

Then, one day, disaster struck. A heavy rainstorm caused a nearby river to flood, putting Zaheer's home and all his belongings at risk. Despite his efforts to save everything, the floodwaters rose too quickly. Zaheer watched helplessly as his prized possessions were swept away.

Meanwhile, Daya, with her minimalistic approach to life, easily protected her belongings, which were few but meaningful.

Daya seems to be
having fun in the rain, but
what about
Zaheer and his things?

As Zaheer stood amidst the wreckage of his washed-away possessions, he realized the stupidity of his excessive shopping.

From that day on, he vowed to be more mindful of what he bought, focusing only on the things that truly brought him happiness and value. And with Daya's guidance, he learned that sometimes, less really is more!

The story of Zaheer
shows us that true happiness
comes from enjoying fun and
love, not from having lots of
unncesessary things!

Chapter 4

The Twitter Tortoise and the Speedy Hare

Deep in the lively forest of Aranya Van, there lived a wise tortoise named Tiku and a speedy hare named Harsh. They were both excited to join a grand race organized by the wise old owl, Guruji. What made this race special was that the participants had to share updates on Twitter as they raced through the forest.

When the race began, Harsh zoomed ahead, sure that his speed would guarantee him victory. He started looking at random stuff on Twitter, feeling like he had already won. But

Twitter
is like a big playground
where you can share your
thoughts with lots of people
and make new friends!

Tiku, true to his nature, took things slow and steady. He kept in touch with the other racers on Twitter, sharing his thoughts and encouragement along the way.

As the race went on, Harsh couldn't resist showing off on Twitter. He boasted about his lead and posted flashy pictures, while Tiku shared wise words and positive messages and observations about the forest.

Halfway through the race, Harsh decided to take a Twitter break. Many animals had commented on his Tweet. Some even congratulated him before finishing the race! He got caught up in all the attention and lost track of time, replying to every comment and message. Meanwhile, Tiku kept plodding along steadily, noticing Harsh's distraction but staying focused on the race.

As Harsh finally resumed the race, he was shocked to see Tiku closing in.

Huh, why is Harsh on his phone?
Shouldn't he be running in the race right now? Can he still win?

Panicked, Harsh tried to regain his lead, tweeting frantically. Meanwhile, Tiku tweeted, "Slow and steady wins the race. Believe in yourself and never give up! #BeWise #PatiencePrevails."

In the end, as the animals eagerly awaited the outcome, Tiku crossed the finish line just before Harsh. The forest erupted in cheers for Tiku's victory, and Guruji praised his wisdom and determination. Harsh felt embarrassed about his overconfidence and learned an important lesson about humility and the power of patience and perseverance.

The story of Harsh teaches us to be patient and consistent, like the tortoise, because slow and steady wins the race!

Chapter 5

The Google Snake and the Doctor Mongoose

Under the tall trees of Aranya Van, there lived a caring mongoose named Dr. Mira and a tricky snake named Shakti. Dr. Mira spent her days caring for sick animals, while Shakti, well, he liked to play tricks to make some easy coins.

One day, Dr. Mira noticed many animals falling ill. When Dr. Mira examined the patients, she was able to identify the true underlying cause. She discovered that Shakti was behind it all! Shakti had set up a website selling a fake cure called "Shakti Snake Oil," claiming it could heal everything from sniffles to

Google
is like a wise old owl that knows the answers to all your questions and helps you find anything you need!

broken bones. Poor animals, hoping for a cure, bought the oil, not knowing it was just a big hoax that could even make them sicker.

Dr. Mira, deeply concerned, was determined to stop Shakti's mischief. She gathered all the animals and told them the truth about the snake oil. She shared stories of those who had gotten hurt by it and reminded everyone about the importance of real medicine that actually works.

The animals were angry and wanted justice. So, they came up with a clever plan. They pretended to order lots of Shakti Snake Oil using fake names and addresses. Shakti was thrilled by all the orders and borrowed money to make more oil. But when he finished making it, the animals revealed their trick, showing everyone Shakti's lies and leaving him trapped in debt.

Shakti's scam was busted, and he was

Luckily, Dr. Mira is here to help, but how will she save the Jungle from Shakti?

sent to jail. He felt terrible for what he'd done and realized the pain he'd caused the animals who trusted him. Meanwhile, the animals celebrated their victory, thankful to Dr. Mira for protecting them from Shakti's sneaky tricks. And from then on, they all knew to be careful and stick to real medicine, just like Dr. Mira taught them.

The story of Shakti teaches us to be cautious and trust only the right information before believing in anything!

Chapter 6

The Maps Bison
and the
Lost Lamb

In the lively jungle of Aranya Van, there lived a wise old bison named Bhim. Bhim was known far and wide for his deep understanding of the jungle and his knack for guiding lost animals back to safety.

One sunny day, a curious lamb named Laddoo wandered away from his flock and stumbled upon Bhim. Laddoo had heard about a magical app called "Google Maps" that could help find the way through any unknown place. Eager to try it out, Laddoo asked Bhim if he could show him how to use it. Bhim smiled

Maps
is like a magical compass
that helps you explore the
world and find your way to
exciting places!

gently and said, "Ah, young Laddoo, technology is useful, but the wisdom of the jungle is precious too." However, Laddoo really wanted to use Google Maps and didn't want to listen to Bhim's advice. So, he decided to go on his own.

Laddoo quickly opened Google Maps on his smartphone and typed in the destination. Without any hesitation, he followed the directions, trusting the app to guide him through the dense forest and across rivers. He saw a sign that said "Do Not Enter," but Laddoo ignored it and kept following the app. Little did he know he was heading straight into the territory of Raja, the fierce tiger.

Suddenly, Raja came up from behind and scared Laddoo with a menacing growl. Laddoo panicked, realizing that his blind trust in technology had led him into a dangerous situation. However, Bhim stepped forward calmly, who had been secretly following Laddoo to protect

Oh no! Laddoo is walking alone in the dangerous jungle. Let's hope he reaches his destination safely!

him! He addressed Raja respectfully, "Raja, Laddoo was misguided by the app. Please, spare us and let us find another way."
Raja, amused by Laddoo's embarrassing situation, said, "You foolish creature! You have trespassed into my territory, but I will grant you mercy this time. Give me your wool for the harsh winters, Laddoo, and I'll let you leave."

Laddoo offered his wool to Raja, and then they turned back, following Bhim's wise guidance. Together, they found a safer path and reached their destination. Laddoo thanked Bhim for protecting him, realizing the importance of jungle wisdom alongside modern technology. From that day on, Laddoo learned to use Google Maps cautiously, always remembering to trust both technology and the wisdom of the jungle.

The story of Laddoo teaches us that listening to wise advice from others helps us make smarter choices and figure out new things easier!

Chapter 7

The Instagram Fox
and the
Innocent Goat

In the bustling world of social media in Aranya Van, there lived a clever fox named Fanakar and an innocent goat named Gauri. Fanakar was known for his cunning ways, always looking for unaware prey to trick for his own gain. He was quite the expert at using Instagram. Gauri, on the other hand, was new to Instagram.

One day, Gauri got a message from Fanakar. "Hey there, Gauri! You've got such a wonderful presence. I have an idea for you," he said. Curious, Gauri replied, "Thank you, Fanakar. What's

Instagram
is like a colorful scrapbook
where you can share your favorite moments with friends
and discover amazing new
adventures!

your idea?" Fanakar responded, "I can see you becoming a big star on social media. I can help you get more followers. Just follow my lead."

Gauri thought it sounded promising. As they talked more, Fanakar gained Gauri's trust. He convinced her to share personal details like her location and even bank account information, promising to help with promotions and sponsorships. But Fanakar's real plan was to use her information for his own shady schemes.

Little did Fanakar know, Gauri wasn't as innocent as she seemed. She was actually quite clever and had a secret mission to stop social media predators. Trained by a cybersecurity organization, she knew just how to spot and expose them.

When Gauri finally gathered enough evidence against Fanakar, she revealed her true identity. "You underestimated

Uh-oh, Gauri doesn't look so innocent as we thought.
Who could she really be?

me, Fanakar. I've known about your tricks all along," she declared. Fanakar was stunned. "How... how did you find out?" he stuttered. With a smile, Gauri replied, "I'm an agent working to stop predators like you. Your deceitful days are over." Gauri reported Fanakar to the authorities, who quickly took action. Justice was served, and Fanakar's sneaky ways were brought into the light for all to see.

Gauri, hailed as a hero, continued to use her social media presence to raise awareness about online safety and the importance of staying vigilant in the digital world.

The story of Fanakar
teaches us to be careful
in life and stand up against
bullies, keeping everyone safe
from harm!

Chapter 8

The LinkedIn Ant
and the
Lazy Grasshopper

Deep in the heart of Aranya Van, there was a tiny ant named Anu. Anu knew that getting ready for winter was serious business. She worked hard to gather food and build cozy shelters for her ant friends. But she wished she had more help.

Then one day, Anu discovered something amazing called LinkedIn. It was like a magical network where she could connect with other ants. She shared her plans and invited them to join in. All the ants were excited to help, and responded positively to Anu's invitation

LinkedIn
is a special place where people connect, share their skills, and find exciting new opportunities!

on LinkedIn, expressing interest in collaborating for the colony's benefit. However, there was an interesting character... Gajodhar, the lazy grasshopper.

While Anu and her friends tirelessly gathered food, prepared shelter, and stored supplies, Gajodhar lounged in the sun, enjoying the present moment without a care for the future and posting silly jokes on LinkedIn. Anu knew they needed everyone's help, so she gave Gajodhar an important job: building tunnels before the snowstorm.

But Gajodhar just goofed off. As days passed, Gajodhar made little progress, boasting on LinkedIn and finding distractions. Gajodhar's laziness prevailed, and the tunnel remained unfinished. One day, a heavy storm struck unexpectedly, and Gajodhar found himself trapped! He was consumed by fear and crying out for help in the darkness.

Gajodhar is fast asleep,
but he needs to dig a tunnel
before the snowstorm comes.
Will he finish in time?

Anu wasted no time. She called for help on LinkedIn, and all the ants rushed to rescue Gajodhar. Under Anu's leadership, they worked together to save Gajodhar from the serious situation.

Safe and sound, Gajodhar realized his mistake. He saw how his laziness had put everyone in danger. From that day on, he promised to work hard and do his part. With Anu's guidance, Gajodhar became a helpful member of the ant community, learning the value of teamwork and responsibility. And together, they faced every challenge that came their way, making Aranya Van a happier and safer place for all its creatures.

The story of Gajodhar teaches us that when we push laziness aside and work together, we can achieve incredible things and inspire others!

Chapter 9

The YouTube Elephant and the Jealous Giraffe

In the vibrant Aranya Van jungle, there was a big-hearted elephant named Airawat. He was loved by all for his kindness and talent. Airawat stumbled upon something magical called the internet and discovered a place called YouTube. Excited to share his adventures, he started his own channel called "The Elephants' World."

Airawat's videos were filled with laughter, learning, and amazing tales from the jungle. Every animal eagerly awaited his new uploads. But amidst all the joy, there was a giraffe named

YouTube
is like a personal theater
where you can watch all your
favorite shows, learn new
things, and share adventures
with friends!

Gigi. She was pretty but felt a twinge of envy seeing Airawat's popularity grow because she had always considered herself the most beautiful and admired animal in the jungle. So, she decided to start her own channel, "The Glam Giraffe," hoping to outshine him.

However, Gigi faced a tough time getting views and followers. Feeling frustrated, she resorted to a not-so-nice plan. She offered rewards to animals to say mean things about Airawat's videos. Soon, Airawat noticed the increase in negativity.

Despite the hurtful comments, Airawat stayed determined to spread happiness. He made a special video called "Spreading Positivity Together," praising even those who had been unkind. He also praised Gigi for her grace and kindness, highlighting Gigi's generous acts of helping others, like offering leaves from tall trees to those in need. This unexpected kindness touched the

Oh no! It looks like Gigi is secretly planning something. Let's hope Airawat's YouTube channel doesn't get into trouble!

hearts of many, including some of Gigi's followers.

Seeing the positive impact, Gigi realized her mistake. She reached out to Airawat, apologizing sincerely. She also acknowledged the positive impact Airawat was making in the jungle. Airawat forgave her and they decided to work together on a new video called "Celebrating Unity and Kindness." They shared stories of animals helping each other, showing the power of coming together.

Their video was a hit! Animals from all over the jungle joined in, spreading love and kindness. Gigi learned that when we put aside our differences and work together, we can create something truly wonderful. And from that day on, their channels thrived with positivity and friendship.

The story of Gigi teaches us to celebrate everyone's goodness and uniqueness, making a world where negativity fades away!

Chapter 10

The Tech Animals
and the
Worried Aranya Van

Once upon a time, in the magical jungle of Aranya Van, something peculiar happened. The animals there were so busy with their gadgets that they forgot to look around at the beautiful world.

Foxes, goats, crows, and monkeys were always on social media, like Instagram and Whatsapp. Meanwhile, tortoises, hares, snakes, mongooses, giraffes, and elephants were lost in platforms like Twitter or YouTube. Even bears, ants, and grasshoppers preferred chatting on Zoom and LinkedIn instead of exploring

What's going on? Why are the animals running and looking so terrified?

nature. This made the jungle very worried!

One sunny day, while the animals were staring at their screens, a tiny spark started a big fire deep in the jungle. The flames spread quickly, turning the lush green jungle into ashes. The animals, seeing their home destroyed, felt very scared and sad. They tried to ask for help using their phones, but the fire made the network go down, and they couldn't call anyone. The sound of animals running filled the air.

In the middle of the chaos, Guruji, the wise old owl, took charge. He called all the animals to a safe place away from the fire. Startled by Guruji's urgency, the animals left their phones behind and hurried to safety. With Guruji's help, they formed a line and passed buckets of water from the river to put out the fire. They worked together bravely until the fire was gone.

Fingers crossed the brave animals stay safe and make the fire go away!

When the flames finally died down, the animals saw how much damage the fire had caused. Suddenly, a strong wind blew through the jungle, making the leaves rustle and the branches sway. It felt like the jungle was speaking to them. The animals heard a voice.

There was Aranya God himself surrounded by the ancient spirits. He said, "Oh, dear creatures, look around and see what happened. Once, the vibrant colors of the flowers, the gentle sway of the trees, and the melodies of the birds have come to a standstill. This is the real world, and needs to be embraced and appreciated."

The animals realized that they had been so busy with their gadgets that they forgot about the beauty of nature. They knew they had to protect their home and learn from the jungle's wisdom. Exploring, they encountered natural wonders, from butterfly flights to roaring waterfalls, filling them with

Whoa, see that?
A huge face is floating in the sky!

awe and reminding them of the beauty they'd missed. They understood how important it was to keep the balance of nature.

Changed by their experiences, the animals decided to use technology wisely and spend more time in nature. Aranya Van became even more vibrant, and knowing that true happiness comes from reconnecting with nature, the animals lived happily ever after.

Until one day, when...

In the end,
while Technology is fun, it's
important to take breaks for
outdoor play, reading, art, and
family time to enjoy a fun
and balanced life!

Acknowledgements

I want to say a big thank you to my Mom for always listening carefully and sharing her joyful laughter, to my Brother for his clever ideas that helped the story grow, and to my wise Friend for checking every detail with patience and care. Their support and help made this book possible, and I dedicate it to them with lots of love and thanks.